PREZ'S PROPERTY

AN MC ROMANCE

SAINTS & SINNERS MC
BOOK 1

WEST GREENE

For Riley, my reason for everything that I do.

For every reader who sometimes just needs short,
smut-filled books to get them through the day.

Interior Design: Tiff Writes Romance

Cover Design: Tiff Writes Romance

Editing: Tiff Writes Romance

Proofreading: Kimberly Peterson

 Created with Vellum

TRIGGER WARNINGS

The MMC in this book cheats on his wife to be with the FMC.

This is an erotic romance, which means there is MORE SEX than there is plot.

The FMC is a club girl. If you don't like club girls getting happily ever afters, this book is NOT going to be for you.

Dawson grinned at me as he leaned on the bar. I flashed him a flirty smile, leaning over the bar so my tits were more visible. He glanced down and licked his lips for a moment before his eyes flickered back up to me, a smirk playing on his lips. "Let me get a beer, baby girl."

This was the game I played every night. For room and board and a bit of money, I did whatever I could to please the men of this club, whether that meant getting them a beer, making food, spreading my legs, or opening my mouth.

I reached up and ran my fingers over his stubble-covered jaw before I stood back up to my full height, striding over to the fridge in my heels. I bent over, purposefully wiggling my ass in his direction as I grabbed him a beer from the very back, knowing Dawson liked his beers extra cold.

I popped the top off before handing it to him. He flashed me a perfect smile, his teeth white against his olive skin. "Thanks, baby girl." He gripped the back of my neck and pulled my lips to his, planting a quick kiss on them. "You'll make a damn good old lady to one of these men one day," he said before he winked at me and strode off.

I sighed. I highly doubted his words. I'd been working for the club for two years now – little over that, actually – and I had yet to capture a man's attention beyond sex. Seemed like all I was good for was my cunt.

I'd been graced with a slim body and great tits. But that wasn't good for anything outside of a bed. I was still working to prove my worth to one of these men that I could take care of them.

I mean, yeah, the sex was a plus, but I was beginning to crave something on a more intimate level. Sure, I could leave the club whenever I wanted, but this club had taken me in when I had nowhere to go. The club president had given me a room, and I earned my keep by doing whatever was asked of me.

The clubhouse doors swung open, and Elijah walked in. Every head in the room turned to look at him as if some unseen force had pulled their eyes in his direction.

Elijah was the club president, and his body exuded power and dominance. He was married, but it didn't stop me from fantasizing about what it would be like to be his for one night. I knew he wasn't faithful to his wife. I'd seen him take club women to his room, not to mention, I'd also seen him fuck them out in the open.

I was guessing that his wife didn't care so long as she didn't see it happening with her own eyes. I could never be that woman, though. If I caught my husband cheating, I'd probably kill him. To hell with the consequences that may follow.

Tonight, Elijah looked pissed. It didn't surprise me. His bitch of a wife had a way of pissing him off. I didn't know why they were still married. It wasn't like she was even aware of what happened with the club. The woman rarely came around.

Without a word, he strode over to the bar. Thinking he wanted a beer, I quickly reached into the fridge and grabbed one, popping the top off for him. I held it out, but apparently, that wasn't what he wanted.

My eyes widened in surprise when he strode right around the bar and grabbed my wrist in his hand. With my heart hammering in my chest, I quickly set the bottle on the bar top as he led me up the stairs to his apartment.

I swallowed thickly.

Looked like I was getting my one night with the president.

Dear Lord, please do not let his wife find out about this.

2

As soon as we were in his apartment upstairs, he shut the door behind us, flipping the lock right after. I stood still, silently watching as he moved around the room. He eventually stopped near what I assumed was the closet and toed off his boots. Then, he shrugged his cut off, his muscles flexing as he did so.

I bit my lip. God, this man was beautiful. And I was both excited and terrified to be spending a night with him. Because while I knew it would be fucking amazing, I also knew his wife was crazy as hell. Facing her wasn't on my list of things I particularly wanted to do.

And against his wife, I held no grounds.

She could beat my ass, and I couldn't fight back. It was one of the downfalls of being a club bunny.

"Turn around," Elijah told me, his deep, masculine voice sliding around me, his command settling deep in my chest.

Drawing in a deep breath, I turned and faced the plain, wooden door, my heart hammering in my chest. A soft gasp sounded from me when he placed his hands on my bare shoulders. His hands were rough and calloused, and his touch sent tingles down my spine.

"Been eyeing you for a while now, doll," he rumbled from behind me. He brushed my long, blonde hair over one shoulder, and his lips met my skin a moment later. I bit my lip, biting back my moan.

He gripped my leather pants and slid them down my thighs, his palms sliding over the smooth skin of my legs as he did so. Wordlessly, he tapped one ankle and then the other, a silent command for me to lift my feet. I came out of my heels and my pants all at once.

"God, this ass," Elijah muttered, his fingers

digging into the soft flesh as he squeezed it. I moaned.

My breath hitched in my throat when he grabbed the zipper on my bodysuit and slowly pulled it down, his rings cold against my spine. After he pulled it down past my hips, it pooled on the floor with the rest of my clothes.

I squeaked in surprise when his hand suddenly wrapped around my throat, yanking my body back against his firm, muscular one. My eyes fluttered closed, a whimper sounding from my lips when he grasped my tit with his other hand, testing the weight of it before he tweaked my nipple.

"Always wondered if these were real," he mused.

"They're real," I told him, hating that my voice came out shaky. This man was affecting me way too much.

He lowered his head and nipped lightly at my earlobe before sucking it between his teeth. I moaned his name, my hands coming up to grip his forearm. With his other hand, he made a path down my body until he slipped his fingers between my legs, finding my slick heat.

"Already so fucking wet," he growled. He

slapped my pussy. A sound that was a mixture of a sob and a moan ripped from my lips. "Your little cunt is greedy for my cock, isn't it, doll?"

"Yes," I breathlessly answered. I wasn't even ashamed to admit it. I wanted this man to own my body for tonight. I wanted him to do whatever he wanted to me.

I felt more naked than I did without clothes when he stepped back from me. I could *feel* his eyes running over my skin. "Face me. On your knees," he commanded.

I quickly turned to face him and dropped fluidly down to my knees. I watched as he pulled his long-sleeved shirt over his head, revealing all of his tan, tattooed skin and his sinewy muscles. I licked my lips. God, he was even better looking without clothes covering him.

"How bad do you want me in your mouth, Olivia?"

My nipples hardened at the sound of my name coming off his lips. "Bad," I whispered.

He pulled his cock out of his jeans and tapped my lips with them. I flicked my tongue out, licking the little bit of precum from the tip of his shaft. Then, I opened my mouth and invited him in.

"*God*," he groaned, his head falling back on his shoulders for a moment. I wrapped my hand around the base of his dick before sucking him in deeper. He laced his fingers in my hair and began to fuck my mouth, quickly dominating me and using my mouth however he wanted.

I didn't care. I was so wet that I could feel my thighs becoming slick. He growled my name, fucking my mouth harder. Thankfully, I didn't have a gag reflex, so he slid down my throat easily. My eyes watered. Drool slid from the corner of my mouth.

He suddenly pulled out of my mouth, his hand tightening in my hair as he fisted his cock. He pumped once, twice, and then came all over my tits, shouting my name as he did so.

3

Elijah stared down at the mess he created for a moment before he jerked his head in the direction of a closed door. "Bathroom is through there," he told me.

I took my dismissal. Rising to my feet, I walked to his bathroom, not letting his sort of harsh dismissal bother me. I was used to being shoved aside after a man was done with me. I shouldn't have expected Elijah to be any different, especially since he had a wife waiting at home for him.

Fuck.

His fucking wife.

Gritting my teeth against that bitter reminder, I turned on the light and cleaned myself up in his shower really quick. I could hear him moving around in his room, but I refused to look over to see what he was doing.

After I was cleaned up, I quickly dried off and walked out to grab my clothes.

But they were gone.

Frowning, I turned to face Elijah. He was relaxing back on the bed. A smirk tilted his lips. My pussy clenched.

Why did he have to affect me so much?

He beckoned me to him with one finger. "Come here," he commanded.

A little thrill shot through me. He wasn't done yet.

Drawing in a small breath, I walked over to him. He patted his thigh, and taking the hint, I straddled him. "You on birth control?" he asked me.

"Yes," I said. A lot of the men liked to fuck raw, and I didn't want an unwanted pregnancy.

He grabbed his cock. I leaned up on my knees and slid down on him. I hissed a breath through my teeth, my hands flattening on his abs as I slowly slid down on him. He was much larger than what I was used to.

"God, you're so fucking tight," he rumbled. He gripped my hip and rubbed my clit. I moaned, becoming wetter, my muscles loosening as he brought me to an orgasm. "There you go," he praised, his eyes locked on my face.

Then, he yanked me down to him before I could come. I didn't have time to think before he fisted his hand in my hair and gripped my ass with his other hand, holding me down as he began to thrust up into me from below. I clawed at the blankets, moans and pleas falling from my lips. I wanted more all while I was becoming delirious from the number of times I was coming around his cock.

From this angle, Elijah was bumping my clit over and over, and his thick shaft was rubbing that perfect spot inside of me, sending me spiraling headlong into numerous orgasms. My head was spinning. I could barely breathe.

Then, he flipped us over so he was on top, and with his thumb on my clit, he continued fucking me. I shook my head, a sob tearing from my throat. Tears sprang to my eyes. I'd never been fucked so thoroughly in my life.

"Elijah, please," I whimpered. "Too much."

He lowered his lips to mine, taking my mouth in a hot, possessive kiss that sent my mind reeling. Chills danced through my body as he brought me to yet another orgasm, this time coming with me.

4

He slowly pulled out of me, his cum spilling out onto the bed. I was too tired and worn out to care. My temples were pounding, and I felt weak – completely spent and drained.

"Stay," he ordered as he rose off the bed. I watched through slitted eyes as he walked to the bathroom. He came back a minute later with a warm cloth, and he used it to clean me up.

That was more than could be said for the other men I'd fucked. They had left me to clean myself up. It wasn't their job, and once they nutted, they were ordering me out. I knew they didn't mean it to be harsh; they just didn't want us forming attachments where we had no business to.

I yawned, my muscles feeling weak. I'd never had so many orgasms in one night in my life, and we'd barely been fucking for an entire hour. I didn't know how I hadn't died from overstimulation, to be honest.

"Need some rest?" Elijah asked me as he pulled on his jeans.

I rubbed my eyes, getting ready to shake my head, but he had already tugged the comforter from beneath me and draped it over me. "Get some sleep. I'll get one of the girls to cover your place at the bar. I'm pretty sure I fucked you into exhaustion," he said, his lips tilting up at the corners.

I didn't say anything in response, my eyes already sliding closed. This wasn't normal behavior for the men in this club, but I sure as fuck wasn't about to complain.

I was almost completely asleep when his phone suddenly rang on the nightstand. With a low growl, he answered it.

"What?!" he barked into the phone, jerking me completely out of my sleep. I snapped my eyes open, looking up at him in alarm.

His eyes flickered to me, rage and something else flickering in their depths. It was gone before I could pinpoint what the other emotion was. "Whatever, Whitney. Don't fucking start shit, you hear me?"

The sound of his wife's name washed over me like ice-cold water. I was already sliding out of bed when he hung up. I made quick work of grabbing my clothes. "You've got to go," he told me. I thought I saw regret flash in his eyes, but it was gone before I could be one hundred percent sure. "Don't fucking breathe a word of what happened here to anyone, you hear me?" He stepped closer to me. I swallowed thickly. "If you do, it's your fucking ass, we clear?"

I gritted my teeth. "Crystal," I muttered.

Not even embarrassed about my nudity, I strode out of his room, barely refraining from slamming the door shut behind me. Doing that would definitely get me a fucking lashing that I didn't want.

I stormed further up the hall to my room and that time, I *did* slam the door behind me.

"What a fucking dick," I seethed.

5

I looked up from the table I was cleaning when Whitney barged into the club-house, the door slamming roughly against the wall, announcing her presence. I heard one of the other club girls mutter a profanity as she disappeared into the kitchen.

I didn't blame her. Whitney was a bitch, but I had tables to clean.

The club didn't pay me to sit on my ass.

"Elijah!" she yelled, making me cringe. God, her voice was loud and screechy.

I watched as the chapel doors swung open. Elijah stormed out. I winced *for her*. One, you didn't barge into the clubhouse if you weren't a patched member. You walked in with respect, and you kept your fucking head down, even if you were married to one of the members. Two, you sure as fuck didn't shout for one of the members like you'd lost your goddamn mind.

The only time you did was if it was a fucking emergency.

"Someone better be dead," Elijah growled at her as he stormed in her direction.

She threw a bag at his feet. His clothes from yesterday spilled out of it. "Why do your clothes smell like some bitch's cheap perfume?!"

Excuse me? My perfume was *not* cheap.

He gripped her arm so tightly I saw tears spring to her eyes. He yanked her close to him, making her trip over the clothes at his feet. I cast my eyes to the table, not wanting to be caught staring and receive the same kind of lashing. Staring at an altercation between Elijah and Whitney was almost just as bad as being in her position.

"My patience with you has disappeared," he snarled down at her. "Your mom raised you to be a fucking good old lady, and that's what the fuck you need to be, you hear me? You keep your fucking nose where it goddamn belongs.

You wash my clothes without fucking complaint. And you sure as fuck don't barge into *my* goddamn clubhouse like you run shit around here, you hear me?"

She meekly nodded her head. The fight died out of her. He shoved her away from him, and she caught herself on one of the tables. Her lips trembled as a tear slid down her cheek.

I wanted to shake my head. I didn't even feel sorry for her. I mean, yeah, it sucked she got cheated on. I felt bad for that shit, but she knew better. When you signed up to be one of these men's old lady, you signed up to turn a blind eye to the shit they did with club women.

Our lives sucked, but yet, our men took good care of us. And I knew if a woman took care of her man well enough, in turn, his dick would only go in one body: his old lady's.

That meant you kept your head down. You did as you were told. You sure as fuck didn't come into your old man's clubhouse, yelling like you owned the fucking place.

"I suggest you settle the fuck down," Elijah growled at her. "And since you want to fucking barge in here, acting like a goddamn child, you can help the women clean up from the party last night. You know where the fucking kitchen and cleaning supplies are."

With that, he turned on his heel and stormed back into the chapel, not casting me a glance. Thank God for that. He was in a bad fucking mood now, and I didn't feel like dealing with a pissed-off biker.

I watched out of the corner of my eye as Whitney picked up the clothes, sniffling as she did so. She carried them upstairs, and I assumed she was taking them to the prez's room and to probably clean herself up before facing the other women.

"Something interesting on my face?" she sneered at me, suddenly turning to glare at me.

I held my hands up in a surrendering gesture, the cleaning cloth held in my right hand. "No ma'am," I quickly uttered, turning away from her.

"Probably one of the skanky bitches he slept with," she muttered as she walked up the stairs.

I glowered at her back. No wonder he fucking slept around. If I had a dick, I wouldn't want to stick it in her sour pussy either.

Fucking cunt.

I focused back on what I was doing, but when I felt someone's stare on me, I looked up, catching Elijah's gaze. His eyes ran over me, and he licked his lips, an appreciative glint in his eyes.

Dear God, help me.

6

After cleaning up with us, Whitney hung out with some of the club women. I couldn't even begin to imagine the humiliation she was feeling, especially since just about every woman here had fucked Elijah at some point.

I'd file for divorce faster than any man could tell me no.

Yawning, I walked up the stairs to my room, wanting a nap. I was exhausted. I'd barely gotten any sleep the night before, still too wound up and pissed off about Elijah. But now that I'd basically helped clean and scrub down the entire clubhouse, sleep was finally calling my name.

I fully intended to take advantage of it.

I cringed when Whitney laughed. The sound was obnoxious, and it grated on my nerves. It always had. I *hated* when she came around.

I squeaked when Elijah suddenly stepped out of his room, stepping into my path. I swallowed nervously, my heart rate skyrocketing. "Been waiting for you to bring your ass up here for two hours now, Olivia," he rumbled.

I took a shaky step backward. His wife was just downstairs. This wasn't a good idea. In fact, it was a horrible one. If she caught us, I didn't have a fucking leg to stand on.

He reached out and grabbed my upper arms, his hands like gentle, steel bands around my slender arms. "Your wife—"

His expression darkened at the mention of her, making me swallow thickly. "Fuck my wife," he growled. "I want you."

Before I could do or say anything, his lips covered mine. Instantly, I was lost in him. Tingles shot through my body as I linked my arms around his neck. With a muttered curse against my lips, he gripped me beneath my thighs and lifted me up. I linked my legs around him, grinding against his hard cock as he strode further up the hall to my room near the end.

He pushed the door open and stepped inside, kicking it closed behind us. I moaned when he pressed my back against the wooden door, his lips now moving over my neck, nipping and sucking lightly at the skin, darkening it with love bites.

"Elijah," I whimpered. *God, how did he feel so good?*

"Easy," he rasped. "I'm going to take care of you. Just give me time," he mumbled.

He yanked my strapless shirt down and cupped my tits. I arched my back, thrusting my chest forward. He squeezed each tit before twisting and pulling at my nipple. I gasped and grabbed his face, dragging it back to mine so I could taste his lips again.

His tongue tangled with mine as he gently set me on my feet, his fingers making quick work of my clothes. Then, he spun me around. I bent over at my waist, not even having to be told, and wiggled my ass in his direction.

He groaned as he ran his hands over the

globes of my ass. "So fucking perfect," he rasped.

Perfect.

I'd never been called perfect before.

I clenched my eyes shut tightly. I was reading too much into this. He was fucking *married.* And even then, if he wanted me to be his old lady, I'd refuse. He was cheating on his wife while she was in the same damn building. Who's to say he wouldn't do the same to me?

He slid inside of me slowly, both of us savoring the feeling of him filling me. Then, he gripped my hips and began to pound in and out of me. My tits swayed back and forth with each thrust. My hands were flattened against the door, and I was thrusting back on him as hard as he was thrusting into me.

"Elijah, I need – I need—" I gasped, unable to get my words out.

He reached around me and rubbed my clit. I detonated, coming around him. He kept rubbing me, and before I could stop it, I squirted all over him. He groaned my name in appreciation, fucking me even harder. My hands slipped, and I fell forward, the new angle now letting him slide deeper.

"Oh, fuck yes, doll," he rasped. "Don't know why I never fucked you sooner, Olivia."

Fuck, I didn't either because he felt fucking *amazing* inside my cunt.

"More," I pleaded.

And he gave me more. He slid his hands over my back as he pounded in and out of me. Then, he did the last thing I expected.

His thumb probed at my ass. I moaned at the feeling. I hadn't been taken in my ass yet, but if Elijah wanted to fuck my ass, I sure as fuck wasn't going to deny him.

"God, this hole is so fucking *tight*," he groaned.

"Never," I gasped, trembling, "been taken there," I sucked in a sharp breath of air, "before."

He gripped my hips. "That's changing today, doll."

7

Elijah grabbed my bottle of watermelon-scented lube and looked at it thoughtfully. "My brothers don't get you off enough?" he asked, looking at me.

I shrugged. "Not all of them are looking to get a woman off, Elijah," I reminded him.

He shook his head. "Always feels better when a woman comes around my cock. Don't understand men who don't seek that." He strode towards me. "Bend over the bed," he ordered. "You'll want to be comfortable for this."

I drew in a deep breath and did as he ordered. Elijah hadn't been kidding when he said my virgin asshole was going to change today. This man fully intended to take my ass as his own.

Before he could even get the bottle of lube open, a knock sounded on my door. The person on the other side jiggled the door handle, but thankfully, Elijah had been smart enough to lock the door.

"Olivia?" Whitney called out from the hall.

"Fuck," Elijah whispered. He pulled me up from the bed and snatched my robe from my floor where I'd dropped it this morning after my shower. He wrapped it around me. "Fucking get rid of her."

He pressed a hot kiss to my lips before disappearing into my bathroom, hiding behind the shower curtain.

My lips were still tingling from his kiss.

Drawing in a deep breath, I quickly fixed my hair and then walked to the door, opening it as I tightened the sash around my waist. "Yes?" I asked her, leaning on my door frame, my voice very calm for someone who was just fucking her husband.

"Have you seen Elijah by any chance?" she asked me.

I shook my head. "Nope. Haven't seen any of the guys, actually," I told her, which wasn't *entirely* a lie.

She sighed, a sad frown pulling at her lips. "Okay. Thanks anyway."

She walked off back down the hall. I waited until I could hear her downstairs before I shut my door and locked it again. Elijah stepped out of my bathroom and without missing a beat, he grabbed me in his arms, kissing me again as he backed me up towards the bed, his hand pulling at the sash around my waist.

No words were needed between us. He turned me around and pulled my robe off, tossing it to the floor before he pressed his hand to my upper back, bending me over the bed. With one hand, he rubbed lube on my ass, slowly working his fingers in as his other hand played with my clit, his fingers occasionally dipping into my soaked cunt.

I whimpered, needing more. Somehow knowing what I wanted, Elijah began to press the head of his cock into my ass. I tensed. He ran his hand over my back. "Easy, doll. Breathe and relax."

"You're too big," I hissed, my body

becoming tenser as he tried pushing in a little more.

"No," he crooned. "Just relax. Trust me, doll."

I drew in a deep breath, but before I could try to relax, he began to furiously rub my clit. I cried out, my body relaxing into the mattress. He sank fully into my ass. Giving me a moment to adjust to his large size, he ran his hands over my body, pressing kisses to my back.

"Good girl. You're doing so fucking good, doll."

My body *loved* his praise, and honestly, so did my mind. I moaned, my hands clenching the sheets. I felt so *full*. I'd never been this goddamn full in my *life*.

And the way he was praising me? The way he was kind of taking care of me? It was settling deep in my heart.

I was playing a dangerous game with the president.

His hand moved back to my clit as he began to slowly move in and out of my ass. I whimpered, clawing at the comforter on my bed. "God, your ass is so *tight*," he rumbled. "I fucking love your body, doll."

"Fuck me harder," I pleaded, trying to push his sweet words out of my mind.

He did as I wished. He plowed into my ass like a man starved. I drenched his fingers as soon as he dipped them inside my pussy, and it seemed to spur him on even more. His hips smacked against my ass with each thrust. He basically had me pinned to the bed, so I was helpless to do anything but lay there and take everything he was giving me.

"I'm going to—" I panted.

"Now, Olivia," he snarled.

I came hard around his fingers, squirting again. He found his release in my ass a moment later. We lay together, both of us trying to catch our breaths. His heart hammered against my back.

"I'm going to ease out," he told me, his lips brushing the shell of my ear. "Then, I'm going to help you clean up."

I nodded weakly. He slowly eased out of my ass, and then, he swept me up into his arms, carrying me to my bathroom.

8

Once the water in my shower was warm, Elijah stepped inside and gently set me on my feet. Silently, he set about washing my hair and conditioning it, and then he bathed me.

It was so hard not to look deeper into his actions.

I'd never had a man *actually* care for me after sex.

My phone rang in the bedroom. Elijah growled in annoyance. "Call them back after we're done here," he muttered.

I stayed silent, knowing better than to disobey him. Besides, it was probably one of the club girls wanting me to come down and help with something. I didn't have any friends outside of this building.

Elijah finished bathing me and rinsed me off. Then, he wrapped me up in his muscular, tattooed arms and slanted his lips across mine, kissing me soft and slow.

My heart couldn't take this. It was so hard not to read deeper into this entire situation, and he was wrecking my fucking heart.

"I want you to be mine, Olivia," he rasped as he leaned back and looked up at me.

I jerked back from him, my eyes widening in horror. "Yours?" I blurted.

He nodded. I stared at him incredulously. He couldn't be fucking serious.

"You're married!" I hissed at him. Did he forget that fucking fast that he had a fucking wife?

He shrugged. "Don't know if you noticed or not, but she and I aren't on good terms anymore these fucking days."

I gritted my teeth. "So, you want me to be your side piece?" I hissed. He *had* to be fucking kidding me.

He flashed me a smile, and instantly, my

anger melted. I'd *never* seen him smile before, and it fucking disarmed me.

He was fucking *gorgeous* when he smiled like that.

I sighed and rubbed my palms down my face, my heart clenching in my chest. This man already had the power to destroy me. "And if your wife finds out?" I finally asked him.

He leaned his massive shoulder against my shower wall and crossed his arms over his chest. "Let me deal with that," he told me. A bad feeling settled in my gut. This wasn't going to turn out well. I already knew that.

"Am I going to be your only piece of ass, or am I to be expected to turn a blind eye like your wife does?"

His eyes darkened as he ran his eyes over me. "Nah, doll. You don't have shit to worry about. I'll only be fucking you. I don't even fuck my wife." That surprised me. He lightly wrapped his hand around the back of my neck and tugged me closer to him. "But I don't even want to see you flirting with any of my brothers, you hear me?"

I weakly nodded. He kissed me again before he stepped out of the shower, grabbing one of my towels from the cabinet above the toilet. "Need to go deal with my wife," he told me. "But meet me in my apartment tonight after midnight."

With that, he strode from my bathroom.

I was so *fucked*.

I watched him as he quickly got dressed. After, he came back into the bathroom, gripped my chin, and kissed me. "I mean it, doll. Don't leave me waiting. If I have to come after you, I'll spank your perfect ass into submission."

My nipples hardened all while my pussy clenched at his warning.

He kissed me one more time and walked out of my bathroom again. A moment later, I heard my bedroom door shut behind him. I turned the water off and slowly stepped out of the shower. My ass was sore, but my body was well sated.

A moment later, I heard Whitney yelling at Elijah. I shook my head and quickly got dressed. I then blow-dried my hair before heading downstairs. I walked behind the bar and began taking a liquor inventory, trying to ignore their argument. Sleep was going to evade me again; I knew that, so I might as well get some shit done.

I was so going to feel this lack of sleep tomorrow, though.

A moment later, Elijah stormed into the clubhouse. I heard the sound of Whitney flying out of the lot, her tires screeching on the concrete when the door opened. He walked over to the bar, his eyes on me. "Get me something strong, doll."

I grabbed a glass and poured straight Vodka into it, handing it to him. It was his preferred drink when he ordered something strong. He flashed me a grin before raising his glass to me and walking upstairs.

Sighing, I shook my head. Tanner, one of the other club bunnies, gently squeezed my arm. "Just keep your head held high," she whispered to me. I swallowed thickly. "It's all we can do until a man decides they *actually* want to keep us as more than a piece of ass."

I sighed. I hated that she was right.

9

The last couple of weeks had been a whirlwind of fucking the prez behind his wife's back. She was coming around the clubhouse a lot more lately, probably because she'd smelled my perfume on his clothes, but she wasn't going to catch him in the act.

One, Elijah was too damn sneaky for his own good, and two, no one in this club was going to rat him out – not one of the women and *certainly* not one of the brothers that wore a cut on his back.

Our loyalty lied with the president, no matter how fucked up he was.

I leaned over the table to wipe down the

other side, too lazy to walk around. Everyone was still asleep, but I hadn't been able to get any rest last night. I'd tossed and turned until I finally said *fuck it* around four A.M., got a shower, and came down here to start cleaning things up from the night before.

I was torn over this shit with Elijah. He was *married*, for fuck's sake. What in the hell was I thinking, continuously letting him take me to bed and fuck me in positions I hadn't even known my body could move into?

I knew the right thing to do would be to cut him off, but I couldn't bring myself to do it. Every time I finally got the courage, he'd aim that fucking smile at me, and I melted. My armor and defenses completely fell away, and I let that man do whatever he wanted to my body, not even giving a fuck that he was wrecking my heart more and more along the way.

But he'd kept to his word. He hadn't touched another woman. I would know because I heard everything within these walls. Besides, every moment he wasn't dealing with club shit or fighting with his wife, he was either inside of me or asleep beside me.

Last night, he'd been stuck in his room upstairs with his wife because she was being a royal bitch and wouldn't leave.

And that's what had kept me up. I was laying in my own bed, wondering if he was fucking her, too, even though he swore to me numerous times he wasn't touching her again.

But he cheated on her with me. Who's to say he wouldn't do the same to me?

To most of these men, pussy was pussy. Didn't give a fuck where they got it from.

I jumped in surprise when I felt Elijah slide his hands over my hips. "You've been scrubbing that same spot for the last five minutes now," he rumbled in my ear. "What's got you worked up, doll?"

You.

I shook my head. "Nothing," I mumbled instead of the true answer. "I'm fine. I'm just tired. I didn't get much rest last night."

He turned me around to face him. A frown pulled at his lips. He hadn't shaved yet, and dark stubble covered his jaw. It made him look even more rugged and dangerous, and I loved the look on him.

Couldn't help but imagine what that stubble would feel like between my thighs, too.

"What's on your mind, doll?" he asked me.

I huffed and tossed the rag I was cleaning with over into the soapy bucket of water I'd been using. "Did you sleep with her?" I quietly asked him.

He shook his head, understanding passing over his features. "No, babe. I slept in my fucking recliner. My goddamn back is killing me."

I relaxed in his hold. He pressed a kiss to my forehead. "That's what kept you up all night?" he asked me. He tugged me to him. "I gave you my word, Olivia."

"You gave your wife your word, too," I mumbled.

He shook his head. "No, I didn't. We had our own vows, and I did not promise fidelity to her."

I jerked my head up to look at him. He shrugged at me. "What?" he asked. "The fuck do I look like promising not to fuck around on her, and I could barely stand her? I married her as a favor to her parents – nothing more."

I cocked my head to the side. It wasn't my

business to ask why that favor had been asked, so I didn't even bother. I just filed it away into the things that I didn't need to know.

"Will you ever promise fidelity to a woman?" I questioned him.

He inclined his head to me. "I'm promising fidelity to you, aren't I? I haven't broken my word. The only place my dick has been is either in my hand, your mouth, your ass, or your cunt, doll."

My pussy tingled at his words. A smirk tilted his lips. "That turn you on, baby?" he asked me, his voice dropping an octave.

I licked my lips. He leaned his head forward, his lips brushing the shell of my ear. A shiver raced down my spine. "I've been craving you all goddamn night," he rumbled in my ear. He slid his hand between my legs, cupping me through my shorts. "Been wanting to fill this tight cunt with my cock. Fucking had to jack off like a teenage boy again last night, imagining those fucking lips wrapped around me."

I moaned. He sucked lightly on the lobe of my ear. "Tell me you want me, doll," he rasped into my ear. "Tell me how badly you want me to fill you up. I'll fuck you right here on this table, baby. Just fucking tell me."

"I want you bad," I whimpered. I grabbed his face, bringing it to mine. "I want you *everywhere*."

His lips smashed onto mine, cutting off anything else I was going to say to him.

10

He settled me on the edge of the sturdy table behind me and shoved my thighs apart, stepping between them. I linked my ankles behind his back, moaning as I ran my hands over his muscular body.

God, how was it possible that this man could be so perfect?

"Got to be quick, doll. I'm sorry," he rumbled.

I didn't care so long as he was inside of me.

He gripped my shorts and pulled them down my legs, groaning appreciatively when he saw I was wearing a thong. He kissed me again, his tongue probing mine. I clutched tightly at his shoulders.

"Fucking love easy access," he rasped as he shoved my thong to the side and dipped his fingers in my sopping core.

I made quick work of his belt buckle before I pulled his thick shaft out of his jeans. Impatiently, he batted my hands away, shoved my thong to the side again, and slid deep inside of me.

He covered my mouth with his hand as I cried out. "God, you're so fucking loud," he groaned before he kissed me, fucking me with punishing thrusts. All I could do was grip his cut and kiss him back, allowing him to keep me quiet all while he bruised my pelvic bone.

As soon as I came around him, he came with me, groaning into our kiss, his hips jerking against mine as he soaked my walls with his cum.

The sound of movement upstairs had him cursing and moving back from me, his cum leaking out of me.

"Fuck, that's a pretty sight," he groaned as he bent to pick my shorts up off the floor.

"You made a mess," I muttered, keeping my voice low so whoever was up wouldn't hear us.

He flashed me that perfect grin that always melted my insides. "I like cleaning you up, too." He gave me a quick kiss as he quickly helped me into my shorts. "Wish I could spend the time to do it today."

He backed up from me just as Wren stepped downstairs, shrugging his cut onto his shoulders. He inclined his head to us. "Your old lady just came out the room," he said quietly, striding towards the bar where I had a fresh pot of coffee ready for them. He lifted the pot to me. "Thanks, girly."

Elijah muttered a curse when his wife emerged downstairs. I moved away from him, heading towards the stairs to go clean myself up. I was tired. I wanted to sleep, and I wanted some more damn time to myself.

11

Seeing his wife was always like having ice-cold water poured over my head. Just like always, I felt disgusting for sleeping with a married man. And just like always, I vowed I was going to cut shit off with him.

"What a fucking slut," Whitney muttered as she passed me, casting me a disgusted look. I tensed up at her words, my chest tightening with anger.

I wanted to fucking slap her.

But that's what I was. I was a club slut – one who fell into bed with her husband just about fucking daily.

Suck my left nut, bitch.

"You should apologize to Olivia," Wren spoke up.

I paused at the bottom of the stairs, my ears tuned in their direction.

"Why should she apologize?" Elijah asked, his deep, gravelly voice sliding around me like a comforting, thick blanket. I didn't turn to face them – had no reason to.

"She just called Olivia a slut for no damn reason all because she thought no one could hear her. She needs to fucking apologize, prez."

This time, I did turn around, plastering a fake smile on my face. Elijah looked pissed, his hand already wrapped around Whitney's arm. "Olivia?" Elijah asked me.

"It's fine," I said sweetly. "Us women are used to that kind of shit."

With that, I turned around and headed up the stairs, but not before I heard Elijah lay into Whitney. "You don't pay these women, you hear me? You don't have the right to say a goddamn thing to them. You don't even have the right to ask them to throw your fucking trash away for you, am I clear? You're overstepping the fucking boundaries I put in place for you. I suggest you step back in that box I put you in, Whitney."

Bitch.

I passed Tanner on the stairs. She eyed downstairs nervously. "Is it safe?" she asked me.

I nodded. "Just avoid the queen," I told her. "She's in a foul-ass mood."

Tanner shot me a knowing smile. "If my husband was sleeping with a woman that looks even half as good as you do, bitch, I'd be pissed, too." I laughed. She squeezed my hand. "Just keep your chin up, girl. That's all women like us can do."

With that, she finished walking downstairs. I sighed and went on up to my room to get a shower and crash in bed, sleep calling my name the longer I was awake.

12

Someone was gently shaking me, and if they didn't fucking stop, I was going to chop their fingers off.

"Go away," I mumbled, swatting at the hand.

Elijah's husky laugh met my ears. "Wanted to come check on you, doll. You've been up here for hours. Thought I'd have a chance to say bye before I left on this run."

I slowly opened my eyes, blinking up at him. My room was still dark, which was one thing I liked about Elijah. He didn't turn the lights on when someone was sleeping.

Or, at least, he didn't turn the lights on

when I was sleeping. I didn't know about anyone else.

"Run?" I groggily asked, trying to get my mind to catch up with what was happening.

He nodded, brushing my blonde hair back off my cheek. "Yeah, doll. Going to be gone a couple of days – three at most."

I slowly sat up and leaned forward, letting my lips mold to his. He groaned and laid me back on the bed, moving over me as he did so. "Door," I mumbled.

"Already locked, doll," he rumbled against my skin as he moved his lips down my neck, pushing the strap of my tank top aside to fully access my shoulder.

I pushed his cut off his shoulders. It didn't take long before we were both completely naked. His lips molded to my breast as he dipped two fingers inside of my pussy, his thumb rubbing my clit. I moaned his name, my fingers tangling in his hair.

"Prez, we're running late," I heard the VP – Jackson – call from the other side of the door.

"Fuck," Elijah muttered. He stood up and dragged my hips to the edge of the bed before sliding inside of me. Again, our sex was quick, but Elijah rubbed my clit the entire time, sending me spiraling into a multitude of orgasms – so many I was struggling to figure out how to suck air into my deprived lungs.

"Elijah," I whimpered, gasping for air.

He growled my name as he came inside of me, soaking my pussy with his cum. He quickly pulled out, watching as his cum slipped out of me. With a small shake of his head, he leaned over me and pressed his lips to my forehead, holding them there as I sucked in ragged breaths of air.

"Easy, doll," he soothed. He ran his hand down my side. "You okay?"

I weakly nodded my head. He kissed me. "I need to go. Get cleaned up and get some more rest, yeah? I told Tanner to let the other girls know you're not to be bothered."

"Thanks," I mumbled, not even sure if I had the energy to get up and clean myself up.

He kissed me again. "Three days – tops," he promised me.

Yawning, I nodded. He stood up and got dressed. Then, he grabbed my hand, pressed a kiss to my palm, and dipped out of my room. A minute later, I heard bikes rumble to life in the lot, and then, Elijah was gone.

13

I had a feeling Whitney was beginning to suspect something was really going on between me and her husband because the moment I emerged from my room after the prez had left, she'd been casting me dirty as fuck looks.

I had been doing my best to ignore her and stay out of her way. If there was one thing I knew about a woman scorned, she would lash out. And it was my ass if I retaliated.

But like fuck would I lay down and take whatever shit she spewed at me if she did. If it meant I got kicked out of here, then so be it. I had enough money saved up to get me by for a couple of months.

Dawson smiled at me as he leaned on the bar. "Let me get a beer, darlin'."

I set down the cloth I'd been using to wipe down the glasses and reached into the fridge, grabbing him a beer. I popped the top off with my lighter, too lazy to walk to the other end of the bar to grab the bottle opener. I handed it to him.

"Prez's old lady looks ready to murder you," he told me.

I sighed. "I know," I grumbled. And I was avoiding her like the fucking plague.

He ducked his head so his eyes met mine. "None of us men are blind to what you two are doing," he said, talking about me and the prez, "and I know you're not the only one in that shit, but you do know if she lashes out at you, there's nothing you can do, right? She ranks above you."

I sighed, gritting my teeth. "Trust me, I fucking know."

He shook his head. "You're dumb to let a man ever make you feel second best, sweetheart."

I flashed him a sickly sweet smile. "You offering to claim me, Dawson?"

He laughed, shaking his head. "Nah. Trying to work Tanner down, but that woman is something else."

I lightly smacked him with my towel before I grabbed a glass and began wiping the water spots off of it. "Maybe if you stop sticking your dick in every piece of available pussy around here, you'd make some headway."

He snorted and swallowed a mouthful of beer. "If she stopped letting every man stick a dick in her, we'd make some headway," he retorted back at me, sort of using my words against me.

I shrugged. "Remember who we are, though, Dawson. We're at *your* beck and call. You want her to stop sleeping with the other brothers? You've got to make it known you're trying to claim her."

He sighed, eyeing me for a moment before he spoke again. "When the fuck did you become so wise, darlin'?"

I shrugged. "Probably when I started getting used as a piece of ass, but yet, I'm not allowed to sleep with other men either."

Dawson shook his head and stood up from his bar stool. "You deserve more, girly."

With that, he strode away.

I know, Dawson. I know.

I WAS EMERGING from the bathroom when Whitney cornered me.

Fuck.

I wasn't prepared to fucking deal with her yet.

"What – no quickie in the bathroom?" she sneered at me.

I gritted my teeth so I wouldn't lash back at her. Stepping to the side, I moved to walk around her, but she blocked me, crossing her arms over her chest.

Here we fucking go.

"You think I don't fucking know about you and *my* husband, Olivia?" she snapped. "That perfume you fucking wear is *very* distinct."

"You don't know a damn thing," I spit at her, finally having enough of her shit.

She shoved me back a full step. I clenched my fists so I wouldn't bash her face against the wall for touching me. I was a fighter, and I *hated* laying down and taking whatever she dished out to me. "You keep your goddamn hands to yourself, you fucking trashy whore. He's *my* husband."

"We're not doing anything!" I shouted at her, finally losing my cool. I didn't give a single fuck for lying to her. "Whatever fucking issues you've got with your husband, you need to fucking take up with him like a goddamn woman instead of lashing out at other women all because you're insecure in your fucking marriage!" I stepped up close to her as Dawson and James rushed around the corner. "And for your fucking information, Tanner and Brit also use the same fucking perfume I do. I would know since we fucking bought the same kind at the same fucking time."

With that, I stormed around her, shoulder checking her. James already has his phone to his ear.

It took everything in me not to lash out at him for tattle-tailing like a little bitch to his fucking president.

"Sorry, sweetheart," Dawson whispered as I stormed past him. "Club rules."

I gritted my teeth and continued walking out of the hallway.

Fuck your goddamn club rules.

14

I lit the blunt, inhaling, letting it settle in my lungs before I blew it out. After finding me scrubbing the tables so hard I was surprised I wasn't fucking sanding them down, Dawson handed me a blunt and sent me out here to smoke and chill out.

My phone rang beside me. With a sigh, I grabbed it, my gut twisting at the sight of Elijah's name on my screen.

Christ.

I did *not* have the energy to deal with his shit right now.

I was half tempted to ignore it, but I knew that would just make the entire situation worse.

Sighing, I swiped my thumb across the screen, pulling my phone up to my ear. "Hello?"

"*What the fuck were you thinking*?" he roared into the phone. His voice was so loud that I snatched the phone away from my ear, flinching at the volume.

"She started with me," I snapped at him when I had the phone back to my ear, not even giving a fuck that I was talking to the president anymore. I didn't give a fuck if he ended everything between us right then and booted me out of the club, firing me.

"And you know the goddamn rules!" he barked at me.

I scoffed. "Are you fucking serious?" I blurted. "You expected me to just lay down and let her say whatever the fuck she wanted to me?"

"If you'd just *called* me afterward like I have told *each* of you to fucking do, I would have handled it," he snarled.

That time, I fucking laughed. "*Handle it*?" I asked. I laughed again. "You mean like you've been handling her so far?" He growled in warning, but I was beyond the point of giving a shit. "Good job at that, by the way. She's *totally* reined in and under your control."

"You're treading on thin fucking ice, doll," he silkily warned.

I inhaled on the blunt, staring out at the darkening sky. "You know what, *Prez*?" I sneered his title. I heard something break on his end of the phone. "*Fuck. You.* We're done, you hear me?"

"Olivia-!" he barked, but it was too late.

I had already hung up the phone.

Good fucking riddance.

15

Dawson knocked on my open apartment door. I was sprawled across my bed, a bit high, but not high enough to deal with anyone.

"What the fuck did you say to him?" Dawson asked me when I turned my head to look at him.

I sat up. "That we were done." I cocked my head to stare at him. Dawson looked wary. "Why?"

"He just cut the run short. He's on his way home now."

"*Fuck*," I swore. A president didn't cut his run short for shit, and the fact that he was on his way home early meant I was in a world of shit. I slid off my bed, shooing him away. "I'm not going to be here when he gets home. I'm done with his stupid bullshit, and I'm not standing by, being made out to be the only bad person in this entire situation."

Dawson sighed. "He'll come after you, Olivia. I've never known him to cut a run short. Club comes first for him. You know that."

I snorted. "I wish him luck in finding me," I retorted as I snatched my duffel bag from the top of my closet.

With a shake of his head, Dawson left my room. He couldn't force me to stay, and he knew that. The club didn't own me, and I didn't wear a man's cut on my back.

WHEN DAWSON HAD SAID that Elijah was on his way home, I hadn't thought to ask how close.

And I should have.

I was packing the last of my clothes into the bag when I heard the bikes ride onto the lot.

"Oh, God, no," I groaned, thunking my head against the wall.

"What the *fuck* did I tell you about keeping

your goddamn head down?!" I heard Elijah bark at Whitney. "The women who work here are *my* problem! You got a problem with one of them, you fucking take it up with me! You keep your goddamn mouth shut around them!"

"Elijah—"

"Go the fuck home!" he barked at her. It was silent for a moment, the only sound being Whitney shutting the clubhouse door as he left. "Olivia!" Elijah bellowed from the bottom of the stairs.

My gut plummeted to my feet.

Shit. Shit. Shit.

I heard his boots pounding up the stairs. I rushed to close my door, but he beat me to it, shoving it open when I pushed against it. He stalked inside and slammed it shut, flipping the lock.

I swallowed thickly.

"I don't know who the *fuck* you think you are," he seethed as he stepped towards me, "but I'm about to fucking remind you where you stand with me, doll."

Dear Lord, please help me.

16

"Elijah," I whispered, a pleading note to my voice. He gripped my arm and yanked me close to him before steering me towards the bed. I swallowed nervously, my heart hammering against my breastbone.

Now that my high had worn off as well as some of my rage, I knew I'd handled the entire situation wrong.

I had been more than aware of the rules surrounding me, keeping me in a tight, neat box. And I'd completely disregarded every single one of those rules when I'd lashed out at not only his wife but at him as well.

He suddenly stopped moving, his eyes focused on my duffel bag behind me. Abruptly, he released me, his eyes swinging back to mine.

"You're leaving?" he asked, sounding shocked.

I jerkily nodded my head. "I was planning on being gone before you came home," I confessed.

He turned away from me and paced the length of my room, shoving his fingers through his messy, dark hair. I watched him warily, unsure of what was going to happen now that he knew I'd been planning on leaving not just him, but this club as well.

"Fuck," he groaned as he turned to face me. "Christ. Don't leave, doll," he pleaded.

I frowned at him. That hadn't been the reaction I'd been expecting. In fact, it looked like he wasn't even pissed anymore. Instead, he was looking at me like he was about to lose his security blanket.

"Elijah, this is becoming too complicated," I told him.

He sighed and scrubbed his massive hands down his face. "I filed for a divorce last week."

My lips parted softly in shock. I hadn't known that. "My guess is she got served papers today, so she lashed out at you."

I frowned. "Elijah, why are you divorcing her?" I asked him.

He sighed. "Why the fuck *wouldn't* I, doll? Being married to her is a fucking nightmare. My favor to her parents is done. There's no reason for us to remain married. The only reason I did was because I didn't want to deal with the hassle of a divorce." He stepped towards me and cupped my face in his hands. "And I want you. I want to claim you, but I know you well enough to know you won't let me completely have you unless I'm a free man."

I frowned at him, my heart aching enough for the both of us. "Maybe not even then, Elijah. I won't be cheated on by my old man."

He grinned down at me, instantly weakening my resolve. "Who the fuck says I would cheat on you, Olivia?"

I scoffed. "Um, you cheating on your wife does," I retorted.

He shook his head at me, that grin never

leaving his lips. "I'd never cheat on you, doll. I'm fucking hooked on you."

With that, he covered my lips with his, effectively wiping my mind of any argument I'd been planning to make against him.

17

Elijah pulled my tank top over my head and unhooked my bra, letting my breasts spill free. He thumbed my nipples as his tongue danced with mine. I whimpered into his mouth, thrusting my chest further forward, needing him to touch me more.

"I missed you," he groaned as he sucked lightly at the skin of my neck.

Oh, my heart.

I clung to him as he lifted me and laid me out on my bed. He shoved my duffel bag to the floor before he gripped my shorts and pulled them down my legs, yanking my thong off after. I leaned up on my knees and pushed his cut from his shoulders, laying it on the end of my bed before I gripped the hem of his shirt, pulling it over his head.

I slid my tongue up the valley between his abs. He groaned, his hands sliding down my arms. "I missed you, too," I told him, meaning it. Because despite how fucked up our situation was, I *had* missed him.

I unbuckled his belt and pulled his zipper down. He toed out of his boots and let his jeans and boxers drop to the ground. I shot him a sensual smile before I slid the flat of my tongue under his cock from the base all the way to the tip.

"You gonna put my cock in your mouth, doll?" he asked me, his voice more gravelly than usual.

I licked the head of his cock before I wrapped my hand around the base of his cock and slowly took him into my mouth, answering his question without words.

"*Fuck*," he hissed.

He gripped a fistful of my hair and began fucking my mouth, hitting the back of my throat each time. I eagerly sucked at him, and he moaned my name, his hand tightening in my hair.

Before he could come down my throat, he popped out of my mouth and stroked himself a couple of times before he covered my tits in his cum. He *loved* making a mess of me.

"Fucking pretty sight," he rumbled. Then, he dropped to his knees beside the bed, yanked my ass to the edge, shoved my thighs apart, and wrapped his lips around my clit.

I screamed, arching my back off the bed. He slipped two fingers inside of me, finger fucking me as his magical mouth worked wonders on my clit, sending me into a multitude of orgasms.

I clutched his hair in my hands, riding his face. When I came again, he moved over my body. And not giving a shit about his cum on my chest, he pressed our bodies together as he slid deep inside of me.

I wrapped my legs around his waist, lifting my hips each time he thrust into me. He was slower than he normally was and a hell of a lot gentler. He kissed me, almost seeming to make love to me.

His arms were banded around me,

crushing me to him as he rocked in and out of me.

My heart was wrecked. My soul was completely destroyed.

Tears burned at the back of my throat, but I kept them back. I wouldn't cry. I wouldn't be vulnerable in front of him.

"Fucking hate being apart from you," he rumbled against my lips. "I'd take you with me every time I had to leave if I fucking could."

I clutched at him in response, wishing we didn't have his wife standing between us like a gigantic boulder prepared to destroy the both of us.

He leaned up on his elbows, pausing his thrusts as he looked down at me. Cum was smeared across both of our chests, but he wasn't paying that any mind. His eyes were locked on my face.

"Promise me you'll allow me to make all this shit right?" he asked me. "I know I'm a dick. I know I've fucked this all up ten ways to Sunday, but don't walk out on me, doll."

I sighed. "Elijah, I'm a club girl. I'm here for any man's beck and call unless you say otherwise or you terminate my employment," I reminded him.

He clenched his jaw and reached between us to rub my clit. I cried out his name, coming around his cock. He moaned at the feeling. "No one touches you but me, Olivia. I thought I fucking made that clear."

I slowly opened my eyes, looking up at him. "No one but you has touched me in a little over two weeks," I reminded him. "But I'm tired of being second best and competing with a woman you claim you don't even feel shit for."

He sighed. "I'm going to do right by you, Olivia. Just trust me."

With that, he thrust back inside of me, this time truly fucking me. He stood at the edge of the bed, my legs hooked over his shoulders as he pounded in and out of me.

Hated to admit it, but as long as Elijah was touching me, I was helpless to do anything but give him whatever he wanted.

My heart was already his, and I'd been fucked from day one of him dragging me upstairs to his apartment.

18

Elijah had been back for a week now, and to say that we'd spent a fuck ton of time together was an understatement. This man had me with him every spare moment he could, even if we weren't fucking.

I'd never known a man in this club to be clingy, but Elijah? He'd been clinging to me since he had caught me packing to leave the club.

I hated that it made me all warm and fuzzy inside, especially since he was technically still married. It didn't matter that he had filed divorce papers. None of it mattered unless his wife signed them as well.

Otherwise, he would remain married, and I would just remain his side piece.

I groaned when my phone vibrated beside me on the mattress. I had *just* woken up – like I was still coming out of my slumber, and already, someone was fucking bothering me.

I slapped my hand around on the mattress until it landed on my phone. Groggily, I swiped my finger across the screen, punching in my passcode. Elijah's name stared back at me.

Get your fine ass in my room – now.

Sighing, I rolled out of bed and shoved my feet into my slippers as I snatched my robe from the back of my door, tugging it around my frame. I was wearing a pair of panties and a large t-shirt that belonged to him. It was one of the many black t-shirts he owned, and I doubted he even noticed it was missing.

He was leaning against his doorframe when I stepped out of my room. That lazy grin I was coming to love tilted his lips as his eyes roamed my body. "Fucking missed you last night, doll," he rumbled as he reached out and grabbed the front of my robe. His lips met mine in a kiss so hot, my toes curled in my slip-pers. "Fucking can't stand it when other char-ters ride through sometimes, especially when it cuts into my time with you."

It was times like this when he said these sweet words to me that I forgot all about who we were and what we were doing.

He pulled me into his room and kicked the door shut, locking it behind us. He kissed me again as he tugged at the rope holding my robe together, letting it part. I dropped my arms, letting the silky material slide down my arms.

He hummed in appreciation. "Thought I was missing a shirt."

I smiled, my cheeks warming. He'd noticed after all. "Want it back?"

He shook his head as he backed me up towards the bed. "Looks a hell of a lot better on you than it does on me, doll. Keep it. Take any fucking shirt of mine that you want."

When the back of my knees hit the bed, he lifted me up and settled me on the mattress. I moaned when he slid his hands up my thighs, his thumbs grazing over my cunt before he gripped the hem of my panties and pulled them down my legs.

I pulled the shirt I was wearing over my head, leaving my body bare for him, just as he liked. He groaned appreciatively before he shoved my thighs apart and buried his face against my pussy. I cried out his name as he sucked on my clit, but before I could move my hips against his face, he held me still, locking my body down, leaving me completely at his mercy.

I whined his name, my back arching off the bed as an orgasm tore through me, making me lose my breath. I clutched at his hair, gasping for breath. Elijah kept lapping at me, slowly working me down from that high.

I lay panting on his mattress as he stood back up and stripped out of his clothes. With a hazy smile, I opened my arms to him as he moved over me.

As soon as he sank deep inside of me, I wrapped my legs around his hips, meeting him thrust for thrust. He groaned my name into my neck as his thrusts became harder, more powerful. It felt like he was trying to break me all while his arms held me together.

A scream tore from my lips. Elijah clutched my body against his as he quickly found his

release with mine, pumping his hot seed inside
of me. After, he held me in his arms, his heart
hammering against my chest.

"Fucking hell," he finally groaned.

Fucking hell was right.

19

I didn't know how long we laid there for. I must have fallen asleep though because when I woke up, I could hear the shower running, Elijah was standing in front of me, his hand held out like he was getting ready to shake me awake.

I blinked up at him. "What?" I groaned.

There was a tender smile on his face. "You need to get a shower, doll."

I groaned and pulled the blanket over my face. "Leave me alone."

He laughed softly. I shot him a glare when he gripped the top of the blanket and flung it back, leaving my bare body exposed to the cold air in the room.

"Dick," I muttered, though I didn't really mean it. I just wanted to *sleep*. The man always fucked me into exhaustion.

He laughed and scooped me up from the bed, carrying me to the shower. I sighed when the hot water ran over me, my body coming awake even though I didn't want it to.

With the amount of sex Elijah and I had, I needed all the rest I could get. The man had a habit of *always* wearing me out.

"Come on, doll," he coaxed, setting me on my feet but keeping a hand on my hip. "I've got church here soon, and you need to get downstairs and help clean up from last night."

And just like that, I felt like cold water had been thrown over me. It happened a lot with him.

I was nothing more than a club girl, and it wouldn't be long before Elijah had enough of me and moved on. Eventually, they all did. I'd seen women come and go because they fell for a patched member that had no intentions of settling down with them.

They couldn't take the heartbreak.

I almost laughed at myself because even I had almost walked from the club over Elijah.

What a fucking mess.

"Come out of your head, doll," Elijah coaxed, pressing his lips to the shell of my ear. "Shower."

"I could have taken a shower in my own room," I told him.

He turned me to face him, a frown pulling at his lips. "I know that tone of voice by now, Olivia."

I huffed. "You're acting like everything between us is okay, Elijah," I blurted. "But the fact that you so easily reminded me that I have to go downstairs and clean up with the other club women reminded me of my place. I'm your whore – not a goddamn thing more."

I was in a foul mood suddenly, and I was lashing out. I knew that, and I couldn't bring myself to stop. Maybe if I pushed hard enough, he'd make the hard decision for both of us that I couldn't seem to make and end this because I didn't have the strength or the willpower to.

Elijah clenched his jaw. "That's what you think you fucking are to me, Olivia?" he demanded. "How many times do I have to fucking tell you that you're not just some piece of fucking ass to me?" He pushed me back against the shower wall and braced his hands on either side of me, caging me in as he glared down at me with his intense, dark eyes. "I'm trying to keep you out of the crosshairs of my fucking wife. She got served papers, and she's pissed."

I knew that. Hell, I had already been in her line of fire once. "I'm not afraid of your wife, Elijah," I told him. And I wasn't. She couldn't hurt me.

He shook his head. "Maybe you should be. She was raised around this shit, Olivia. And her head hasn't exactly been screwed on straight lately."

I scowled at him. "If you're so worried, then why do you keep pushing this between us?" I asked him.

He dropped his forehead to mine. "Because I can't fucking let go of you, doll." Some of my anger drained out of me at his words. "Believe me, I've thought about it, and each time, the mere thought of not having you fucking guts me." I swallowed thickly. "You're the only woman I'll walk through hell and high water for."

Not giving me a chance to respond, he

kissed me and pushed my thighs apart. I moaned when he lifted me up and slid inside of me, his mouth still on mine. And then, Elijah fucked me slow and steady, and if I wasn't stupid, I would have thought the man was making fucking love to me.

I moaned his name as he sucked at the skin of my neck, marking me as his. I clutched at him, my thighs tightening around his hips as I steadily rose towards that peak, all too eager to go soaring off of it into climactic bliss.

"Elijah," I whimpered, my heart hammering in my chest.

He reached between us and rubbed my clit. "Come for me, doll. Drench my cock, Olivia."

He kissed me as I came around him, my walls clutching at his cock, greedily milking him.

20

As soon as Elijah and I emerged downstairs, his wife walked in the door. A dark growl sounded from Elijah's chest as he moved towards her. She shot a dark look at me, but Dawson stepped up to my side, crossing his arms over his chest.

But we weren't dumb. She wouldn't dare do anything with Elijah in the same room. Problem was though, she now had evidence that Elijah and I were fucking since we'd come downstairs together in the middle of the day.

It was the exact kind of drama I hadn't wanted.

"Church in five," Elijah ordered before he

shoved Whitney in front of him and slammed the doors behind them.

It didn't take long for their argument to reach our ears. With a heavy sigh, I moved behind the bar and snatched up a bar towel, beginning to wipe down some clean glasses so we could put them up.

"Got a feeling shit's going to hit the fan soon," Tanner said, leaning her hip against the counter as she regarded me. "You sure you're ready for that shit storm?"

I shrugged. "Doesn't matter if I am or not. It's going to happen regardless."

She shook her head. "I don't envy your position. Fucking the prez was fun for one night, but you're walking on very thin ice, and I can already hear that ice cracking."

I blew out a soft breath. "You're not the only one," I told her. I'd begun feeling that crack long ago. "I can feel the cold water beneath my feet."

Tanner gently squeezed my wrist and walked into the kitchen, most likely to start doing inventory on food. It was that time of the week. Food shopping on Tuesdays. Liquor and beer run on Thursdays.

Kane walked over to the bar, eyeing me appreciatively. I hadn't seen him in a while. He was a bit of a drifter.

I aimed a smile at him. It was a friendly one, but not flirty. I'd dialed back on my flirting to basically nonexistent since Elijah had staked a claim on me in his own weird way.

"Feel like I don't see your cute ass around anymore," Kane said. "Let me get a beer, darlin', and maybe a good view of your ass while you're at it?" He winked.

I turned, and my attention immediately caught on Elijah. His eyes were narrowed at me and Kane, and his fists were clenched at his sides. I swallowed thickly. He made a move towards us, but Dawson – ever the peacekeeper – stepped in front of him, talking to him quietly.

"Might want to yank the plug on that flirting, brother," Jax told Kane. "She's spoken for."

Kane arched an eyebrow at me. It made sense he wouldn't know. He was more nomad than an actual member, though he wore the patch of this charter.

"By who?"

"Prez," Jax told him.

I flinched when the clubhouse door slammed. Kane frowned and stood from the barstool. "I'll go talk to him, darlin'. Don't worry."

I offered him a weak smile in return as he grabbed his beer, heading for the clubhouse doors. Jax gave me a small smile. "They'll sort it; don't worry. You weren't in the wrong." He shrugged. "Besides, shit's got to be confusing for you. Prez has claimed you, but he's still got you down here working, serving all of us."

"Glad I'm not the only one a bit lost," I muttered. "He says he's protecting me."

"From that crazy fucking wife of his, I assume," Jax said. He tapped the bar. "Elijah knows what he's doing, even if what the two of you are doing is a bit fucked up." I frowned, casting my eyes to the counter. "But trust him, yeah? Prez is a man of his word."

With that, he strode away, leaving me to my thoughts. I stared at the clubhouse doors for a moment.

Was Elijah really that good of a man, though, or was I just setting myself up for heartbreak in the long run?

He hadn't promised fidelity to his wife, so

what would make him promise fidelity to me? Not only that but even after they divorced, there would be nothing tying Elijah to me.

He would be a free man in a world full of available pussy.

And that shit stung more than I wanted it to.

Truth of the matter was, I was in deep, and despite Elijah's words to me, I didn't trust them one hundred percent. He'd cheated on his wife with me. Not a damn thing would stop history from repeating itself even if he did claim me.

I wanted to believe in the exact opposite, but I wasn't a little girl. I'd seen and heard way too much working for this club. As an old lady, yeah, you moved up in the ranks, but your man's word and orders were still all that mattered. And if you were ordered to shut the fuck up and deal with what he was doing behind your back? Well, that's just what you fucking did.

"Seriously, how hard is it to fucking wash the goddamn sink out?" I growled under my breath as I scrubbed at what looked to be toothpaste.

Probably from one of the club girls who had to come brush her teeth after getting her mouth bathed in cum. We were all guilty of having to do it at one point or another.

"It's cute as hell when you talk to yourself, doll," Elijah said from the doorway, surprising me.

I jerked upright, swinging my eyes to his. A smirk played on his lips that had my belly twisting with need. That smirk meant only one thing; he wanted me.

He backed me further into the bathroom and closed the door behind us. I stepped into him, my hands coming up to grip his cut as he lowered his mouth to mine.

"Fuck, I've missed you," he groaned.

I laughed softly because honestly, I had missed him, too. "You just had me this morning," I murmured against his lips.

He groaned and lifted me onto the freshly cleaned countertop. "I want you with me all the time," he rasped, his lips moving down my neck. I angled my head back, granting him more access. He rewarded me by sucking on one of my soft spots. I moaned his name, sliding my fingers into his hair.

He slid his hands under my shirt and gripped the edges, pulling it over my head before he unclasped my bra, tossing it aside as well. His hands cupped my breasts before his mouth descended on one of my nipples, sucking it into his mouth, his tongue flicking back and forth over the tight peak.

I whined his name, pushing at his cut, wanting him naked as well. He kissed me hard, his hand pulling at my hair. "You're so fucking impatient," he growled at me.

I shot him a sexy smile in return. With a small shake of his head, he gripped the edge of my shorts and yanked them down, tearing my panties off after them. Then, he pulled his cock out of his jeans and slid inside of me.

"I wanted you naked," I told him, moaning afterward.

"Too bad," he retorted, a grin playing on his lips. He crushed me to him, sliding in and out of my soaked cunt. "Too desperate to be inside of you."

I cried out his name as an orgasm unexpectedly washed over me . . .

Just as the bathroom door swung open.

Elijah didn't stop. He reached down and rubbed my clit, his eyes on whoever was standing in the doorway.

"Get the fuck out," he snarled at whoever it was.

"I knew you were fucking her!" Whitney screeched.

I snapped my eyes open, stilling, reality washing over me. Elijah gripped the back of my neck and rubbed my clit harder, sending me spiraling into yet another orgasm. I tried to bite back my moan, but I couldn't. "I said *get the fuck out!*" he roared.

The bathroom door slammed shut a moment later. Elijah kissed me hard and fucked me like a man possessed, his hips slamming against mine so hard I knew I would have bruises. But I welcomed the way he was with me.

He wasn't in control. He lost himself in me.

When he came, he crushed his mouth to mine again, his hand pulling at my hair, leaving me completely at his mercy.

22

Elijah cupped my face in his hands once I was dressed again, his dark eyes boring into mine. "Can I convince you to stay in this bathroom while I deal with her?" he asked me. There was real concern in his eyes, as well as worry for my well-being.

I shook my head, swallowing thickly. "Is it worth it?" I asked him. "The drama, the fight that's about to happen – is it worth it?"

"Worth every goddamn bit," he told me. "You're it for me, woman." My heart swelled in my chest. "I want you – just you. I haven't even looked at another woman since I had you in my bed that very first time."

I stared up at him, shocked by his words. Men like Elijah, men that wore the cut of this club – they didn't say that kind of shit. "You mean that?"

He nodded. "I don't say shit I don't mean, Olivia. You should know that by now. A brother's word is all we've fucking got."

I wrapped my arms around his neck and leaned up on my tiptoes, pressing my lips to his. "Then let's go out and face the music."

He crushed me to him. "I really don't want you out there. She's fucking fuming."

I shook my head at him. I wasn't a coward, and I didn't run from my problems. I certainly wasn't going to hide behind a man, either. "If she was going to do anything, she would have done it while you were balls deep in my pussy and rubbing my clit."

He laughed softly and shook his head before grabbing my hand in his, leading me from the bathroom. His body was slightly in front of mine, a protective move I didn't miss. It warmed my soul to know he really wanted this with me.

Whitney was pacing when we stepped out into the main room. Tanner was standing at the bar, Dawson standing beside her. His gun was laid out on the counter in front of him.

I tightened my hand around Elijah's. If Dawson had his weapon out, that meant trouble – serious fucking trouble.

"Who the *fuck* do you think you are?!" Whitney shouted. She stormed over to us. Elijah blocked her. "Move! This fucking cunt—"

"Watch your goddamn mouth about her," Elijah snarled at his wife.

Whitney laughed. It was cold and malicious, and it sent chills down my spine. "You protective over this whore? You know how many of these men have stuck their dicks inside of her? To be honest, Elijah, you were probably the last man of this club to get in her loose cunt."

Elijah released my hand and shoved her a step back. She pulled out a gun and aimed it at me. I drew in a deep breath, forcing myself to remain calm. I tilted my chin up at her, willing my hands not to shake.

Every man in the room, Elijah included, pointed their own weapons at her. "You going to shoot me, Whitney?" I taunted her. Elijah cast me a dark look, a warning for me to shut my mouth. I didn't heed it. "You could never satisfy him, honey."

She stepped towards me, anger flashing in her gaze as she momentarily became distracted. Elijah took that moment to disarm her, shoving her down to the floor on her knees, her wrists bound in his hand as he pressed the barrel of his gun to the center of her forehead.

"I called your parents this morning," he told her, his voice low and quiet. Yet, it still held the threat of death. "They know I've filed divorce papers, and I also informed them that you're not cooperating. They should be here within the next couple of hours." Whitney's face paled. "You'll go home with them, Whitney. You'll sign those divorce papers. And you won't fucking show back up at my goddamn clubhouse or on my territory ever again, you hear me?"

He crouched down in front of her, shoving the barrel of his gun in her mouth. Tears slid down her cheeks. "And if you fucking *ever* threaten Olivia again, I'll tear you apart piece by fucking piece and let you bleed out slowly at my goddamn feet."

With that, he stood up and shoved her down to the floor. "Get out, Whitney."

She scrambled up from the floor and rushed for the door, tears streaking down her face. Elijah put his weapon back in the holster beneath his cut. "Dawson, Jax, follow her. Make sure she doesn't take shit that doesn't belong to her, and get her the fuck off my territory."

23

Being with Elijah apparently meant I got special privileges – like being in the chapel. Normally, the chapel was forbidden. If any of us women got to clean in the chapel, it was with at least two members inside the room, watching our every move.

I understood it. All of us understood it. These men couldn't take any chances that we would put something in the room that could incriminate them.

But today, Elijah had allowed me in the chapel *by myself* to clean it.

I had honestly stared at him for a good minute, trying to figure out if he was playing some sick prank on me. But when he just pressed a kiss to my forehead and strode off outside, the rest of the men following him, I knew he wasn't.

He actually trusted me that much, and that shit warmed my soul.

He and Whitney had been separated for a good few months now. She hadn't been around, though Elijah had to go to a shit ton of divorce hearings. Apparently, Whitney was trying to claim infidelity, but with no proof, she was shit out of luck.

But a couple of days ago, the divorce had been finalized, and Elijah walked away with everything, just as he'd wanted. And he was already in the process of selling their house and her car. I'd asked him why, but he simply said he wanted to start off fresh with me – didn't want me in anything they used to share.

Hell, he had even had all the furniture in his apartment upstairs thrown out and had replaced it with all new shit.

And in the process, without my permission, he'd moved all my shit into his room.

That had been a pretty ugly fight, but he'd won and fucked me into submission. Hell, he had fucked me so good that he could have put me in a tent outside, and I probably wouldn't have cared.

The man was a fucking sex god.

And I'd somehow ended up doing old lady shit without having the title of an old lady, but damn, the man pleased me so well that I didn't even give a shit.

How sad was that?

I was wiping down the table when Elijah made an appearance. He stepped into the room, shutting the doors behind him. My nipples hardened on reflex when he flipped the lock into place, making sure we wouldn't be disturbed.

A lock only meant one thing. This man wanted time alone with me, between my legs, and he didn't want to be disturbed.

I coyly smiled at him as I set my cloth aside. "Where do you want me?"

He grinned. "Fucking love how well you know me, baby girl, but I've got a question for you first."

I frowned, suddenly on guard. "Okay, shoot."

He stuffed his hands in the pockets of his jeans, blowing out a soft breath. He almost seemed . . . nervous. But that couldn't be right. Elijah wasn't the kind of man to get nervous.

"I want to claim you – officially," he told me. "No more club girl status. You're mine – one hundred percent. I take care of you – of every need you have." My heart skipped a beat in my chest. This almost seemed too good to be true. "You'll wear my name on your skin where every other bastard can see it, and you answer to me – only to me."

I rubbed my palms on my shorts. "You mean that?" I asked him. This seemed almost too good to be true.

He nodded. "With every fiber of my being, doll. I want you to be completely mine."

I moved around the table to stand in front of him, putting only about a foot of distance between us. "No cheating?"

He shook his head. "I'll write a goddamn statement promising you fidelity and sign it if you want me to. I don't want anyone else but you, doll. You're *more* than enough for me," he promised.

I hopped onto the table, beckoning him towards me with a finger. "Then I suggest you get busy claiming your old lady."

24

With a growl, Elijah stepped towards me and shoved my thighs apart, coming to stand between them. He gripped my hair in his fist and yanked my head back, covering my mouth with his. I moaned into the kiss, my hands coming up to grip his cut, tugging him even closer to me.

"I'm taking your ass today," he rasped as he moved his lips over my jaw, sucking at my earlobe before he moved down my neck.

I moaned, grinding against him. "Take me however you want me," I told him. A gasp ripped from my lips when he shoved my tank top down with my bra cups, palming my tit in his hand. "I'm yours."

"Damn fucking right, you are." He lowered his head and pulled my nipple into his mouth. "I plan to worship you to the point you're begging me to stop."

"Doubt you could ever get me to that point," I whispered, clutching his head against my chest, my fingers tugging on the soft, dark strands of his hair. I loved fucking him just as much as he loved fucking me.

Which was quite a bit.

He pulled my shirt over my head before unhooking my bra, tossing it to the floor. He worshipped my chest, his tongue laving over my nipples, his massive hands and fingers squeezing the tender flesh, sending shockwaves of pleasure straight to my core.

I rubbed against him, desperately needing friction. I needed *something*. I felt empty, my core clenching. Just from the stimulation of my nipples, I was on the verge of coming.

He leaned up and yanked my shorts and panties down my legs before shoving his fingers inside of me, his thumb working my clit as he moved his mouth back to my breasts. I came within moments, screaming his name, my body trembling on the sweaty table that I'd just cleaned.

I squeaked when he dragged me to the edge of the table and spun me around. Using my cum, he lubed up my ass and his cock before he played with my clit, sinking deep into my tight ass.

"Fuck," he groaned, slowly easing inside of me. I whimpered, my hands flat on the table, nothing to grip. He felt so good inside of me, and with his fingers working my clit, I was on the verge of coming again. "I'll never get over how *tight* this perfect ass is."

He moaned when he settled deep inside of me. He gave me a minute to adjust before he slipped his fingers inside of me, finger fucking me as he took my ass. He started slow, letting my body fully get used to him before he began to pound in and out of me.

I had no doubt my screams reached beyond the chapel, but I didn't give a fuck.

Elijah had just claimed me as his old lady, and that meant the whole goddamn world to me.

25

When we emerged from the chapel, Tanner shot a knowing smirk in my direction. My hair was a fucking mess, and my legs and ass were sore. Walking was definitely a bit of a task, but I managed, not a hint of shame on my face.

Elijah turned me to face him once everyone turned to look at us. He covered my lips with his, kissing me slow and deep before he looked at everyone else. "She agreed to be my fucking old lady!" he cheered.

A party ensued from there.

Music pounded through the speakers. Tanner began to serve drinks. Elijah didn't even bother grabbing a beer. He just dragged me to the makeshift dance floor. Our bodies moved together to the upbeat music, both of us becoming highly turned on by the way our bodies were moving together.

His mouth found mine as he gripped my ass in his hands, hauling me closer, both of us grinding together. Our tongues danced just as erotically as our bodies, intertwining in a hot as hell tangle.

"Take me," I begged him, my hands sliding under his shirt.

"Doll, we're not going to make it to my fucking room," he warned me, his dark eyes meeting mine before he kissed me again.

"I don't care." I moaned when he palmed my breast, squeezing the tender flesh roughly. "Fuck me here. I don't give two shits if everyone watches. I'm yours." I smiled coyly at him, using his jealousy against him. "It's not some-thing everyone hasn't seen before."

That got him.

With a growl, he spun me around to face the nearest table. My shorts dropped within a few seconds, and then he sank deep into my cunt, his hand pulling at my hair as he fucked me like the savage he was known to be.

"Fuck yeah!" Tanner cheered. Then, I saw Dawson settle her on the bar and strip her from her jeans before fucking her as well.

I became lost in the sensations of Elijah pounding in and out of my sopping pussy, claiming me in one of the only ways he knew how.

And this man? He was definitely staking his claim. He was letting every man know in the fucking building that I was now untouchable by everyone except him.

"Elijah," I moaned, getting so close. "I need—"

He circled my clit with his fingers. I screamed his name, clutching the sides of the table as we both found our releases, his cum shooting deep into my cunt, coating my walls with his seed.

He pressed his lips to the back of my neck, his breath fanning over my skin as he panted. "Mine," he rumbled, not able to utter much else.

I nodded, my heart racing so hard and so

fast that I could feel the beat of it within my teeth.

I completely belonged to the president, and I couldn't have fucking been happier.

I stumbled into Elijah, giggling as I did so. It was the first time I'd been able to join in on all the drinking festivities, and I was *wasted*.

Elijah laughed softly as he wrapped his arm around me, holding me up before I slumped to the floor.

"I think you've had a bit too much to drink, doll," he told me, shaking his head, a smile playing on his lips.

"Just a little," I giggled, squeezing my fingers together. Hell, I apparently had two hands wavering in front of me doing the same motion, so it was fair to say I was way past drunk.

He laughed and leaned down, sweeping me up into his arms. "I think it's time to call it a night, doll."

I pouted at him. "Do we have to?"

He grinned. "Yeah, doll. You've had *way* too much to drink."

I pouted. He leaned down and kissed me, licking the seam of my lips. "Mmm. Strawberry."

I beamed at him. "Tanner made it. It tastes *really* good."

He shook his head, nodding at some of the men as he passed them on his way to the stairs. "It's probably what got you fucked up, too."

Once we were upstairs, he laid me on the bed. I groaned and rolled onto my side, yawning.

"Not yet, doll. Come on. You need to get changed into something more comfortable," Elijah coaxed.

I groaned. "No. Leave me 'lone," I mumbled, sleep already tugging at me, slurring my words even more than they already were.

He flipped me over onto my back. I groaned in protest. He kissed me softly before he tugged my shirt over my head and unsnapped my bra, tossing both items to the floor. I pulled at my nipples, moaning as I did so.

"Not tonight, baby girl," Elijah gently told me as he tugged my shorts down my legs. "I want you sober every time I take your body."

I whined in protest. He laughed softly and pressed a kiss to my inner thigh before he pulled his shirt over his head and slid it on me. I rolled back onto my side as he walked over to a dresser, letting my eyes slide shut.

I groaned in protest again when Elijah gently rolled me back over. "Come on, doll. Let's get these panties on you, and then you can sleep."

I huffed but obeyed, yawning again. Once I was dressed completely, Elijah slid in bed behind me, tugging me into his arms. He turned off the lamp and pressed his lips to the back of my head. "Goodnight, baby girl."

"Night," I mumbled, but I wasn't sure if it was coherent. Sleep was already pulling me under.

27

I felt like miners were hacking away at my skull.

Definitely not the best way to wake up.

I groaned and reached up to hold my head, my eyes slowly opening. The room was dark. Elijah's arm was still thrown over my waist, but I could tell he was awake. Hell, I was shocked that he was still in bed considering he was normally up and dealing with club shit right about now.

"How bad is the hangover?" he whispered.

I sighed. "Horrible," I muttered.

He pressed a tender kiss to the back of my head before he got up from the bed. I heard him move into the bathroom. I shut my eyes again, listening as he quietly opened and closed a door and ran some water.

A moment later, he was kneeling in front of me, a glass of water in one hand and two tablets in the other. "Take these," he ordered. "We'll get a shower, get some greasy food in your stomach, and get you hydrated. You'll feel better by noon; I promise."

I slowly sat up, nausea swirling in my gut as I did so. I moaned in discomfort, squeezing my eyes shut, willing myself not to vomit all over Elijah's bed.

"Easy, doll," he rumbled. "Open."

I obediently opened my mouth, and he dropped the two tablets in before pressing the glass of water to my lips. I greedily drank the entire glass, my throat way more parched than I thought it had been.

After, Elijah helped me up from the bed and led me over to the bathroom where he proceeded to undress me. I let him lead me through the motions, lifting my arms when he told me to, stepping out of my panties when he tapped my ankles.

And then, he bathed me in the shower,

gently washing my hair for me before soaping my entire body down. He didn't even push for sex, though I knew he wanted it considering his cock was bobbing between us, desperate to be inside me.

Instead, Elijah focused on taking care of me, and it was really fucking nice.

TANNER SET a plate of greasy fries in front of me with two bottles of water. "Fries?" I questioned. It was time for *breakfast*, not lunch.

"Trust me – they're hangover miracles," she assured me. "You got pretty fucking wasted last night."

I groaned. My head was still pounding, but the guys had drawn the curtains in the clubhouse, shrouding it in darkness besides a lamp here or there turned on so no one walked into any tables.

"Remind me to never drink this much again," I mumbled.

Elijah laughed softly beside me, a cup of coffee in his hands. "Eat, doll."

I frowned at the fries. "I'm not sure if I can hold this down," I confessed.

His hand splayed over my bare thigh, and he gently squeezed it. "Just try."

With a heavy sigh, I grabbed a fry and popped it in my mouth, chewing slowly. My stomach was still churning, but I didn't feel like vomiting, so I guess that was a plus.

Dawson took a seat on the other side of me, nodding once at Tanner. She flushed and rushed into the kitchen. Elijah chuckled. "Still can't pin her down?" Elijah asked him before he took a sip of his coffee.

"Woman is as stubborn as they fucking come," Dawson complained.

"Stop sticking your dick in every hole available in this clubhouse, and you might make some leeway with her," I mumbled, feeling particularly grouchy. Besides, it wasn't fair to call Tanner stubborn when he wouldn't be straight up with her.

Dawson grunted at me. "Not fucking just one woman until she gives me exclusivity as well."

I shrugged and grabbed another fry. "Her job is to spread her legs when asked. You want exclusivity with her? *You*," I said, pointing the fry at him, wincing when pain shot through my skull, "have to make that happen."

Dawson stayed silent. I shoved the fry in my mouth and dropped my head to my hand, closing my eyes as I chewed. Elijah silently rubbed my back. Tanner popped out of the kitchen with a plate of eggs and toast for Dawson and a cup of coffee. She set both items in front of him. Then, before she could walk away, he grabbed her wrist and yanked her down to his lap, covering her lips with his.

I grinned at them before I closed my eyes again, finishing up my plate of fries.

Maybe one day they'd have what Elijah and I shared together.

28

Tanner was on a fucking rampage, and I was the one she was venting to since I knew how she felt.

Dawson had staked a claim on her in front of every member of the club before he strode into the chapel for church a few minutes ago.

She scrubbed at a ring on the table beside the one I was wiping down. Anger burned in her eyes. "Can you believe the fucking audacity of that asshole?" she sneered.

I sighed. "These men work in mysterious ways," I reminded her. "Hell, Elijah staked a claim on me, and he was fucking *married*." That shit still made me a bit bitter.

Tanner huffed. "Fucking men. Like, he

wants me all to himself, but is he going to keep his dick out of every other bitch here that wants to fuck him?"

I didn't have an answer for her because unfortunately, not even old ladies had any say-so in what their men did. Even I just had to have faith that Elijah wouldn't fuck around on me.

Though, considering how much my man loved to be between my thighs, I doubted I'd ever have that issue.

I sighed. "Just got to go along with it, Tanner," I softly reminded her. "It's that or leave the club." I reminded her. Her face screwed up in distaste. For whatever reason, she wasn't keen on leaving this club, and I knew it had nothing to do with Dawson.

Poor woman was hiding from something.

I moved on to the next table as Tanner pondered my words. I sprayed bleach on it and was wiping it down when the chapel doors opened. I looked up, watching as the men filed out, my man the last one to emerge from the room.

He narrowed his eyes at me when he saw that I was cleaning. I frowned and set down the cloth and spray bottle in my hand, my heart thumping wildly in my chest as he stormed in my direction. "The fuck are you doing, Olivia?" he demanded.

Now, I was extremely confused. "I'm cleaning," I told him in a sort of *duh* tone.

I squeaked in shock when he knelt and threw me over his shoulder, striding for the stairs. "Elijah!" I yelled. "Put me down! What in the hell did I do?!"

He smacked my ass, and I squeaked in shock, biting my lip to also hold back my moan. I didn't get an answer from him. Instead, when we stepped inside our room, he set me on my feet and kicked the door shut before turning his dark gaze on me.

"Strip. On your knees."

Obediently, I did as he ordered, my pussy now soaked. I was already wet from him throwing me over his shoulder and smacking my ass, but when he went into this dom mode he had, I was more than ready for him to pummel the fuck out of my cunt.

As soon as I was naked, I dropped down to my knees for him. He stripped out of his own clothes before gripping his massive cock, stroking it a few times as he stared down at me, running his eyes over my tits. They were heaving up and down as I breathed, my body more than ready for whatever he was about to do to me.

Finally, he gripped my hair, tilting my head back some. "Open."

I parted my lips, and he slid his thick shaft into my mouth. I moaned and reached up, gripping the end of his cock, swallowing him down as much as I could. Then, I proceeded to give him one of the best blow jobs of his life, my mouth making slurping noises as I bobbed my head back and forth, moaning when he tightened his hand in my hair.

"God, I fucking love your mouth," he rasped, his dark, glittering gaze on mine.

I massaged his balls in response, rubbing my thighs together as I worked on getting him off. He moaned, his eyes momentarily shutting before he snapped them back open. "I'm going to cum down your throat, doll. Swallow it like the greedy little bitch you are."

Hot spurts of his seed spilled down my throat. I greedily drank him down, not letting a single drop slip from my lips. He pulled out afterward and dragged me up to my feet, his mouth covering mine, not even giving a shit that his cock had just been stuffed in my mouth.

"Your mouth is a gift from God," he swore.

29

Elijah let me go and walked around me. I turned, following him with my eyes. "You don't clean anymore," he told me.

I frowned. "That's what I've always done, Elijah. I don't expect special treatment since you laid a claim on me."

He sighed in annoyance, turning to face me again. We were both still naked, but naked or not, the man still oozed power and dominance. "Not special treatment, doll. As my old lady, your duties change. You keep the club women in line. You make sure that they're doing what they're supposed to do to keep my men taken care of."

I crossed my arms over my chest. His eyes dropped to my tits for a moment before they settled back on my face, our gazes clashing. "Your wife sure as fuck didn't do that."

He grunted. "My *ex*-wife," he said, stressing the ex part, "was a selfish bitch who didn't know the first goddamn thing about being an old lady. The only part she seemed to retain from everything her mother taught her was opening her legs when she was told to."

I gritted my teeth at the thought of them fucking. "She never wanted to do what she was supposed to do. So, for years, it's been me keeping all the club women in line."

"And now you expect me to do that?" I demanded. "That's going to cause a shit storm, Elijah."

He gritted his teeth before forcing his jaw to relax. "Any of those women give you shit, you come to me, you hear me? As my old lady, they have to give you the same fucking respect they give me."

With that, he turned into the closet, signaling that the conversation was over. With a huff of agitation, I leaned down to grab my clothes. I was setting them on the bed when

Elijah emerged from the closet holding a leather cut in his hand.

"Does your normal cut need to be washed?" I asked him, frowning at myself. I was already neglecting my duties as his old lady. Damn, I fucking apparently sucked at this shit.

He laughed and strode towards me, shaking his head. "This is yours," he said, turning it around and holding it up for me to see the back.

Tears burned in my eyes. It had the club emblem in the center like all the men wore, but above the emblem, it read *Prez's Property*, and on the bottom, it read *Saints & Sinners MC*.

"Elijah," I croaked, any other words completely lost to me.

"Whitney never got one of these," he told me. "I never wanted her to wear it." He put it on me, holding it so I could thread my arms through the holes. "But you?" He gripped my chin, his other hand gripping the back of my neck. "I want the entire goddamn world to know who the fuck you belong to."

30

He pressed his mouth to mine, kissing me so deeply, so *hungrily*, that I got drunk off of him. My mind completely blanked as I reached up to twine my arms around his neck, leaning up on my tiptoes to press my body against his.

He backed me up until the backs of my knees hit the mattress, and then, he settled me down on it, his body coming down on top of mine.

The leather of my brand new cut was cold against our skin, but we were quickly warming it up as his body pressed mine further into the mattress.

"I love you," he rumbled, leaning up to look

down at me. My lips softly parted in surprise. "Pretty sure I've loved you for a long goddamn time. My eyes have been on you since the moment you walked through my door, asking if I could provide you with room and board in exchange for whatever the hell I needed done around here."

I remembered that day. I had just been kicked out of the apartment that I shared with my ex. When I had found him in our bed cheating, I had trashed the apartment. Cops had been called. I got hit with a fuck ton of fines, which Elijah had taken care of for me when the cops had shown up here to drag me to jail for contempt of court.

"Why didn't you make a move before?" I asked him, honestly curious.

He brushed my hair back. "Because I had a gut feeling that the moment I got a taste of you, I was going to want more and more until I couldn't fucking let you go."

Oh, my fucking heart and soul.

I leaned up and kissed him. "You know, I used to fantasize about what it would be like to be with you – even if it was just for one night?"

He grinned. "You did? I don't feel like I'm so pussy whipped now."

I laughed. He kissed me again before moving over my jaw and down my neck, leaving hickeys on my pale skin before he parted my cut and sucked one nipple into his mouth, his hand massaging and pulling at the other one. I writhed beneath him, moaning his name, pleading for more as I raised my hips off the bed, trying to get some kind of friction.

I moaned when he finally parted my legs further apart and slid deep inside of me, his lips molding to mine once again. He rocked in and out of me, his pace not picking up.

He was making love to me.

"I'm taking you to the courthouse tomorrow," he rasped.

I dug my nails into his back. "You sure you're," I moaned when he bumped my clit, "ready to tie yourself down to another woman?"

He kissed me again, his tongue dancing with mine. "So long as it's you, I don't give a fuck."

He spread my thighs further apart, hooking them around his arms. The new depth and angle had him bumping that sweet spot inside of me, and I came hard around him, my pussy walls fluttering around his cock.

I dragged his face down to mine, forcing our eyes to connect.

"I love you," I whispered, meaning the words from the depth of my soul.

With a growl, he flipped me over to my stomach and proceeded to fuck me hard, his hips driving in and out of me with a punishing force. He leaned over me, his lips at my ear. "I'm keeping you in this bed until you're knocked up," he promised.

Oh, sweet Jesus.

WANT DAWSON AND TANNER?

Snag it here!

https://books2read.com/dawsonsproperty

JOIN MY NEWSLETTER!

Want to stay up-to-date with sales, new releases, new preorders, etc?

Join my newsletter!

FOLLOW THE AUTHOR

Facebook

Instagram

Facebook Group

Mastadon

Twitter

Patreon

Pinterest

MERCH STORE

Access my merch store here.

ABOUT THE AUTHOR

West Greene is a romance author that specializes in short, steamy books and erotic shorts.

All your instalove needs can be found in one of her books, whether you're looking for possessive men, men with no morals, spicy FF romance, a boy just needing his Daddy, a twink just needing love, or even the other woman to get her HEA.

West Greene refuses to be stuck in one trope or type of romance. She loves variety, and she's definitely going to share that variety with her readers.

https://westgreenebooks.com